3 3052 01479 8062

# URGENCY EMERGENCY!
## Little Elephant's Blocked Trunk

For Aimee & Oli

Library of Congress Cataloging-in-Publication data is on file with the publisher.

Text and illustrations copyright © 2009 by Dosh Archer
First published in Great Britain in 2009 by Bloomsbury Publishing Plc.
Published in 2014 by Albert Whitman & Company
ISBN: 978-0-8075-8354-8

All rights reserved. No part of this book may be reproduced or transmitted
in any form or by any means, electronic or mechanical, including photocopying,
recording, or by any information storage and retrieval system,
without permission in writing from the publisher.

Printed in China.
10 9 8 7 6 5 4 3 2 1 NP 18 17 16 15 14

For more information about Albert Whitman & Company,
visit our web site at www.albertwhitman.com.

# URGENCY EMERGENCY!

## Little Elephant's Blocked Trunk

### Dosh Archer

Albert Whitman & Company
Chicago, Illinois

It was a busy morning at City
Hospital. Nurse Percy was helping
Little Jack, who had a plum stuck
on his thumb, and Doctor Glenda
was typing something important
into the computer.

Just then the ambulance arrived.

"Urgency Emergency! Little Elephant with a blocked trunk! We have Little Elephant with a blocked trunk coming through!"

Little Elephant's trunk looked as though it was about to burst. He was very frightened. His mother was with him.

"Let me examine him,"
said Doctor Glenda.

"It is just as I thought—there is something squeezed up his trunk! We must deal with this immediately or it will burst!"

"Little Elephant, can you tell us what is up your trunk?" asked Nurse Percy.
But all Little Elephant could do was cry.

"We need to know what we are dealing with," said Doctor Glenda. "Nurse Percy, we must take an X-ray to find out what is up there before we try to get it out. I will take the X-ray myself."

Nurse Percy gave
Little Elephant some
medicine to make
him feel better.

Then he took Little Elephant to the X-ray room.

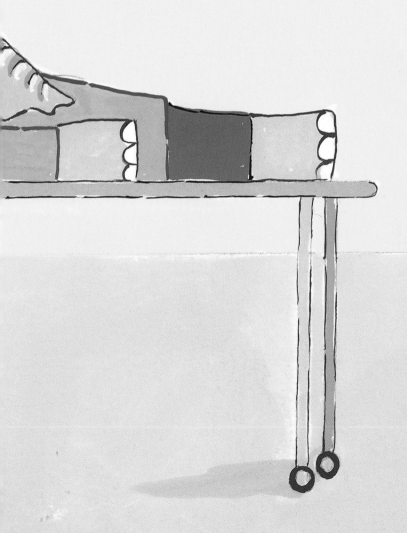

Doctor Glenda took an X-ray picture of Little Elephant's trunk. Little Elephant cheered up when he saw the X-ray machine with all the wires and tubes.

"It is almost impossible to believe," said Doctor Glenda. "How could this have happened?

A ping-pong ball, a pencil, a ruler,
and a toy truck are all stuck up
his trunk."

"Just tell us what happened," said
Nurse Percy to Little Elephant.
"No one will get you into trouble."

"I put the ping-pong ball up first," said Little Elephant, "just to see what would happen. When it wouldn't come out, I tried to get it out with the pencil, and when that got stuck, I tried with the ruler, but that got stuck too."

"What about the toy truck?"
asked Nurse Percy.
"I just wondered if it would
fit," said Little Elephant.

"We can't wait any longer," said Doctor Glenda. "We must remove all the objects as quickly as possible. I will perform the procedure myself. Bring me the Obstruction Suction Machine."

When Little Elephant saw the Obstruction Suction Machine, he started to cry again.

"Don't worry, Little Elephant. It won't hurt a bit," said Nurse Percy.

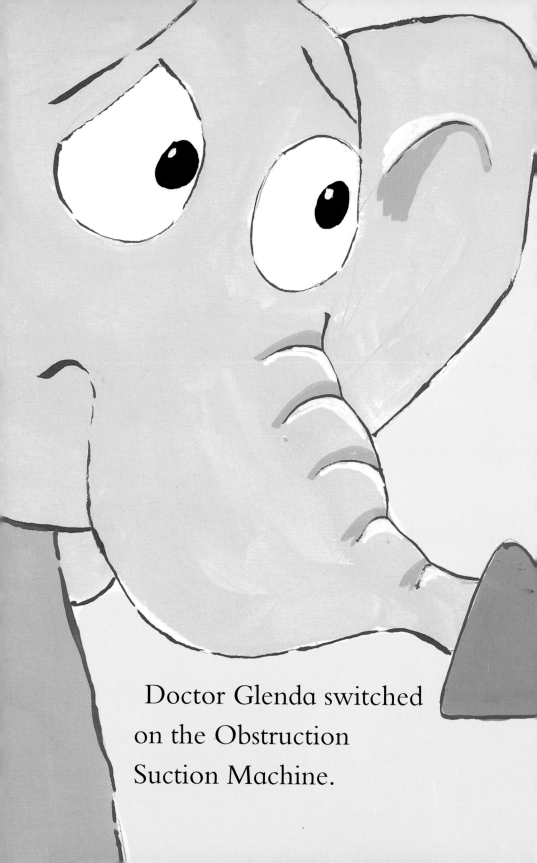

Doctor Glenda switched
on the Obstruction
Suction Machine.

It made a loud whirring noise. She put it on the end of Little Elephant's trunk and they all waited…

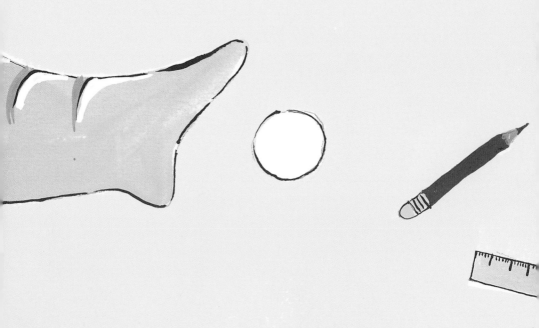

Pop! Pop! Pop! POP!
It sucked out the ping-pong
ball, the pencil, the ruler, and the
toy truck.

Nurse Percy was right. It didn't
hurt a bit.

"That's my best toy truck,"
said Little Elephant. "Can I have
it back?"

Nurse Percy gave it a good wash. "You can, Little Elephant, but remember: NO MORE PUTTING THINGS UP YOUR TRUNK EVER AGAIN."

"I can never thank you enough," said Mrs. Elephant.

"All in a day's work," said Doctor Glenda. "All in a day's work."

Mrs. Elephant took Little Elephant home. Thanks to Doctor Glenda and her team, Little Elephant, his trunk, and his best toy truck were fine.

Enjoy more funny beginning readers in the
# URGENCY EMERGENCY! series...

ISBN: 978-0-8075-8352-4
$12.99/$14.99 Canada

ISBN: 978-0-8075-8358-6
$12.99/$14.99 Canada

"Top-notch medical care in an equally terrific early reader
that will appeal to preschoolers, new readers of all ages,
and anyone else who appreciates droll humor and an inventive plot."
—*Kirkus Reviews* starred review

## ALBERT WHITMAN & COMPANY
*Publishing award-winning children's books since 1919*
www.albertwhitman.com